THE BIRD

WILLOW ROSE

Cover design by Juan Villar Padron,
https://juanjjpadron.wixsite.com/juanpadron

Special thanks to my editor Janell Parque
http://janellparque.blogspot.com/

**To be the first to hear about new releases and bargains
from Willow Rose.**
Sign up to be on the VIP list below.
I promise not to share your email with anyone else, and I
won't clutter your inbox.
- SIGN UP TO BE ON THE VIP LIST HERE:
http://eepurl.com/wcGej

https://www.bookbub.com/authors/willow-rose

Connect with Willow Rose:

willow-rose.net
madamewillowrose@gmail.com

~

"They're coming. They're coming."
- *The Birds, Alfred Hitchcock 1963*

~

1

"Look at the cute birdie, Mommy!"

"What birdie?" Sally yells from the kitchen.

"The birdie sitting in our window," her daughter, Winnie, squeals. "It's sooo cuuute. Come see, Mommy. Come see."

Sally washes her hands, then wipes them on a towel. She walks into the living room, then pauses.

"It's inside? There's a bird inside the house?" she almost yells. Sally has been terrified of birds since childhood when one got stuck in her hair. While other Florida kids feared snakes and roaches, birds were always her thing.

"Oh, my God," she says.

Don't panic, Sally. Don't panic.

"Look, Mommy," Winnie says and points at the small white bird. It is sitting quietly on their windowsill.

"Don't go too close, Winnie."

"Why, Mommy? Why? Uuuhh. Look at those eyes. It has green eyes, Mommy. Isn't it be-au-ti-ful?"

Sally swallows, then nods. She doesn't want to scare her daughter. She doesn't want to bring the same fear into her life that she has suffered from her entire life. So, she tries hard to keep it together. For the sake of the child.

"Just...let's...it must have flown in through the door; maybe we can get it to fly back out, huh?"

"No, Mommy. I don't want it to leave. It's *purdy*. Can we keep it, can we, pleeease?"

Sally cringes at the word purdy. She can't stand it when her daughter doesn't speak properly. She shakes her head energetically. "No. No. I mean...this bird belongs to nature and shouldn't be kept indoors."

"Aw. But it's so purdy."

Again, she cringes. "I know, honey. I know. It's very *pretty*, indeed." She over pronounces the word to make sure her daughter hears the difference.

The bird moves and Sally shrieks. The bird jumps from the windowsill to the dining table. Sally can hardly stand it.

I need to get this thing out of here. Before it gets tangled up in Winnie's hair. Oh, dear God, I can't even stand thinking about it.

Sally waves her hand at it. "Shush."

The bird doesn't move. Winnie is staring at it, fascinated. "Look, Mommy. It's like it's looking at me. The green eyes are looking at me. Hi, little birdie."

The bird moves again. It's jumping, almost sliding towards Winnie. "Stand still," Sally says to her daughter.

The bird jumps onto Winnie's arm and shoulder. Sally lets out a small scream but drowns it out with a clasp to her mouth. The bird is sitting completely still on Winnie's shoulder.

Oh, God, what do I do? What do I do? It's getting closer to her long hair. Her beautiful long hair.

"The broom," she says. "The broom."

She hurries to the kitchen and grabs the broom, then runs towards her daughter.

"Mommy? What are you doing? Mommy? MOMMY!"

Her daughter shouts, but it's too late. Sally swings the broom towards the bird and slams it into it. The bird lets out a squeak, then darts through the air towards the wall, slams against it, and slides to the ground, a few feathers still hanging in the air after it has hit the tiles.

"MOMMY!"

Winnie storms to the bird and kneels next to it. She touches it gently, while Sally calms down, trying hard not to relive the moment the blackbird pulled her hair while clawing her scalp, screeching and screaming to get out.

"Mommy, I think you killed it," Winnie cries and picks it up in her hand. She stands with it and holds it out to her mother, tears streaming across her cheeks. Her crying is maddening to her mother.

"Mommy, Mommy, Mommy, you killed the birdie, you killed the purdy birdie."

Sally approaches her. "Now, now. I...I didn't mean to hurt it. I was just afraid it might...get tangled up in your hair or something."

"Look at the little birdie, Mommy. It's all dead."

And that is when Sally sees it. The bird moves its tail. "No, no," she exclaims, relieved. "Look. It's still alive."

2

Winnie caresses the bird gently on its chest, sobbing. Sally feels awful. She didn't mean to hurt the bird, only get it off her daughter, but her fear got the better of her and she hit it too hard.

"What do we do?" Winnie says, sniffling.

Sally has no idea. She wants that bird out of her house, yesterday. She really doesn't care about one small bird, but she can't disappoint her daughter either. She has always preached to her how important it is to be good to animals.

"Do we take it to the vet, Mommy?"

Sally is in the middle of preparing dinner. She is running behind now on her chores. She has to do the laundry and make a lunchbox for Winnie too. She doesn't really have the time to drive to the animal hospital and sit there and wait for a long time. And for what? One small bird that will probably die anyway?

"Tell you what," she says and walks to her closet. She pulls out the old shoebox that she uses for all her old pictures and letters. She brings the shoebox to Winnie and shows it to her.

"What's that?" Winnie asks.

"A bed. For the birdie to sleep in while it gets better."

"You expect it to sleep in there on the hard floor?"

"It's not...it's a bird...all right?" she says with a growl, then walks to the kitchen, grabs an old cloth, folds it and puts it inside the box. "There, you go. Now it's soft and nice for the little birdie."

Winnie looks inside, then smiles. Carefully, she places the small bird on the soft cloth. She grabs the box and holds it in her arms. "There, there birdie. I'll take good care of you and make you well. No one is going to hurt you ever again."

She gives her mother a look and Sally sighs. "I didn't mean to hurt it, Winnie. I told you."

Winnie looks at the bird, then up at her mother. "How do you take care of a bird?" she asks.

Sally sucks air in between her teeth. James is the one who knows about birds. Mostly because he goes duck hunting when the season is right. He will know more, but she can't really disturb him at work because of some bird in their house, can she? Besides, she really needs to get on with dinner in order for it to be done when James comes home from work. But the look in her daughter's eyes is about to kill her.

"All right," she says. "Let's look it up."

Sally grabs her iPad, then Googles *How to take care of a hurt bird* and finds an article that she thinks sounds good. She reads it.

Winnie sits next to her on the couch. She hasn't cracked the reading code yet, not like the rest of the kids in her Kindergarten class. It worries Sally that she still doesn't read when all the other kids do.

"What does it say?" Winnie asks.

Normally, Sally would let her try and read it herself,

helping her to sound out the words, but there simply isn't time for it now. So, Sally reads out loud to her instead.

"Put the bird in a box lined with a soft cotton cloth or paper towel—did that," she says with a smile, happy that she did something right. "Then close the lid and place the box in a dark, quiet, safe place for an hour or two. The bird likely has a concussion, a build-up of blood under the skull, pressing on the brain." Sally looks at the bird and then remembers how it was swung through the air and slammed against the wall. Yes, a concussion is probably the right diagnosis. The question now is if it will ever wake up from it or if she has actually killed a cute little bird in front of the very eyes of her five-year-old daughter and traumatized her for life.

What kind of a mother are you?

"Then what?" Winnie asks.

Sally reads on. She skips the part where they talk about the blood draining from the bird's brain and reads the last part: "After an hour or two, take the box safely away from windows, but in an open area, facing woods, brush or another suitable habitat, and open the lid. Let the bird fly away."

Sally stops, then looks at her daughter. Winnie's big eyes are on her.

"And what if it doesn't? Mommy, what if it doesn't fly?"

Sally shuts off the iPad. "Then we'll take it to the vet, okay?"

Winnie sighs and looks down at the bird. "All right."

J ames Ferguson rushes to the gate and stops the Jaguar. He nods at the security guard, who nods back, recognizing him, then opens the gate. James drives onto the island, over the small bridge, enjoying the view over the Intracoastal waters.

He likes living on Lansing Island. As a young kid, he could only dream about ever living there, on the gated island where all the rich people lived, and now after ten years as an investment banker, he has finally made it.

James drives onto the street where some of the neighbor's kids are playing on their bikes and scooters in the middle of the road. James laughs heartily. He loves the fact that Winnie is going to grow up in a place where kids can do that. This is the safest environment you could ever raise a kid in. Nothing gets past the security guard and no one gets onto the island without an appointment and thorough check.

If only Sally wasn't so afraid to let the kid go outside on her own.

It has gotten worse, James thinks. Every year it gets

worse. She didn't used to be like that. She never used to be afraid of things. Now, it's like she can hardly get into a car without squirming in fear that someone might hit them or they might crash. Before they had Winnie, Sally was fear-less. Always the one who would go scuba diving or surfing, but now she is all of a sudden afraid of the ocean and won't even take Winnie to the beach. It annoys James that she has locked herself up like that in the house. It's like she stopped living.

James drives slowly past the kids and waves at them, while they yell, "Hi Mr. Ferguson," before getting back to their activities. He can't help thinking about his poor sister who was kidnapped when she was only eight. She was snatched at the bus stop while waiting for the school bus. He never saw her again. Even though he tried as an adult to track her down, she simply vanished and the police never found out who took her or where she ended up. He has no idea if she is still alive or not.

James drives into the driveway and stops the car with a deep sigh. It feels nice to be home after a long day. He likes what he is doing—don't get him wrong. No, it's just a lot of pressure on his shoulders, handling all this money for all these huge companies. He is constantly afraid of messing up, even though you can't ever tell on his face. He learned that quickly in his business. It's all in the poker face. No matter how bad it looks, you gotta look and make it sound like you've got it under control. More than that. Like you're in charge and nothing can stop you.

It gets exhausting from time to time, but James is getting quite good at pretending.

James pops a piece of nicotine gum and chews it while letting the stress out of his body. He likes to leave it in the car and not bring it with him inside. His daughter and wife shouldn't sense how much the job wears on him. They should be happy and not worry. He does his best to make everything good for them, so the least Sally could do is to be happy and not fearful all the time, right?

He breathes out while still chewing. He's been without cigarettes for two weeks now and this time it seems to be sticking. Usually, at this time of day, he would be sitting in his car smoking a last cigarette while letting all the stress go —one cloud of smoke at a time. But his last visit at the doctor's hadn't been good. His blood pressure was too high and he had a cough that wouldn't let go. Not to mention the sky-high cholesterol for his age and too much intake of alcohol; well, all that kind of makes him on the verge of a heart attack. So, he quit smoking. For Sally and Winnie's sake.

James finishes chewing and as soon as he feels relaxed enough, he spits it out in a paper-towel and wraps it, then gets out of the car and throws it out in the garbage can. He takes in a deep breath and pulls his shoulders back and forth, prepping himself for the second round of poker face today.

He puts on his husband and father-smile, then grabs the door handle and pushes the door open.

"Honey, I'm home," he chirps, making sure to sound like he had the best day of his life.

"I'm in the kitchen," Sally yells back. She comes out in a hurry, kisses him quickly, while wiping her hands on her apron, then returns to the kitchen.

"Daddy!"

Winnie screams and runs towards him. She throws herself at his leg. He lifts her up and hugs her tightly, his heart overwhelmed with love for the little creature. "Hey, baby girl. What have you been up to?"

"We have a bird," she says.

"A bird?"

"Mommy almost killed it."

James chuckles. "She did now, did she?"

"Yes, you should have seen her. She knocked it with the broom and made it fly through the air. Poor, poor birdie."

"I'm sure she didn't mean to hurt the little bird," he says.

"I think she did," Winnie says.

He puts her down with another chuckle. "So, where is this birdie, then?"

She grabs his hand and pulls it. "Come. Come see."

4

W innie lifts the lid of a shoebox and James looks inside. There is actually a real bird in there, he is surprised to realize. Up until now, James believed it was just one of Winnie's many stories, but it is actually there. He can only imagine how bad this must be for Sally, who suffers from severe bird-phobia, or whatever they call it.

"Look, Daddy. It's a girl."

"Is it dead? It looks kind of dead, sweetie."

Winnie shrieks and looks inside. She touches the bird on the wing and it moves slightly.

"It's not dead, Daddy. It's not dead."

"Well, that's swell," he says, looking at his watch. He is starving. "Maybe you should put the lid back on so it can get some rest."

"Mommy said to let it sleep for two hours," Winnie says, determined. "Is it six o'clock yet?"

"As a matter of fact, it's six thirty," he says.

"Shouldn't it be flying, then?" Winnie asks.

James shrugs. "I don't know, baby. Maybe it just needs a little more time, don't you think? Hey, how about you and me go find Daddy's big bird book and see what type it is, huh?"

Her eyes light up. "Yay."

She puts the lid back on and they walk hand in hand into James's office. As a hunter, he has a lot of books about animals. He finds the one on birds, then takes it down and starts to flip the pages.

"I don't think I have ever seen a bird like this one before," he says as he looks for it.

"That's because it's very special," Winnie says.

James chuckles. "I bet it is."

James flips a few pages more, then looks at Winnie, who scans through all the birds on the pages, then shakes her head every time she doesn't see it.

"It kind of reminds me of a hummingbird," James says. "The size at least." He finds the hummingbird and studies the picture.

"That's not it, Daddy. Its beak is different. More curvy. Like a hawk's beak."

"So maybe it's more like a cuckoo, then?" he says and flips a couple of pages more.

Winnie looks at the pictures of the different cuckoos and then shakes her head. "Nope. That's not it either."

"I don't know," he says. "I think it kind of looks a little like it, don't you?"

"You have only seen it while it's asleep," she says.

"True. What can you tell me about it, then?"

"It has green eyes," she says.

James wrinkles his forehead. "Green eyes? What do you mean green eyes?"

She looks up at him. "What I said. It has green eyes."

"Birds don't have green eyes," he says.

"Yeah, they do," she says. She points at a picture in the book. "Like this pelican has blue eyes."

James looks at the picture of the pelican. The eyes are more white or gray to him. "Well, I have never seen a bird with green eyes."

"Birds can have many different eye colors. It even says here that they can also have red eyes," Winnie says and points at the text.

James smiles. He knows how much Sally has fought to help Winnie read. "Did you just read that?"

Winnie chuckles. "Yes, I did. I sounded the words out."

"Good job, baby girl. Good job. Your hard work is finally paying off. Now, let's find this bird. It can't be that hard, now can it?"

5

"It's the oddest thing," James says and passes Sally the steaming potatoes.

"What is?" she asks.

"We looked through the entire book, but we couldn't find this bird anywhere. Pass me the gravy, will you?"

She passes it to him, chewing her chicken. She is getting pretty tired of hearing about this stupid bird and just wants it out of her life.

"Well, that is odd," she says, without meaning it.

"Winnie says it has green eyes. I thought it sounded so strange, so we looked it up and apparently birds can have all kinds of eye colors, even red. Actually, it was Winnie who read that and told me. I guess all your hard work is paying off, huh?"

Sally blushes. She hasn't really been doing everything she is supposed to in order to get Winnie better at reading, but she takes the compliment with a nod.

"Mommy, it's been more than two hours," Winnie suddenly says. "Me and daddy looked at the birdie just before dinner and it didn't get up or fly away like it was '*opposed* to.'"

Her pronunciation makes Sally cringe. She has to restrain herself from correcting her daughter. James doesn't like it when she does it. There is no reason to upset her. He says it will go away on its own. That she'll grow out of it. "Have you ever met an adult who kept saying *opposed to* instead of *supposed to*?"

"Mommy?" Winnie asks, her eyes big and wide, tearing up, almost ready to cry again.

Please, don't cry, baby. Please, don't.

"I'm sure it will fly when you're done with your dinner," Sally says and points to her daughter's plate. "Now, eat."

Winnie leans back in her seat. "I'm not hungry."

Sally sighs and drops her fork. They have been fighting with Winnie for the past many months just to get her to eat. Well, to get her to eat proper, healthy food that is, because when it came to snacking and desserts, she had never lost her appetite. Winnie has become quite overweight the past year or so and the doctor told them to make sure she eats healthy stuff, but Sally can never get her to do it.

"Winnie," she says, putting on her serious mommy-voice. "You have to eat. Remember what the doctor said at our last visit, huh? You must eat your vegetables. Every day. And meat. Meat keeps you full for a longer period of time so you don't eat so much junk."

"I don't want to," Winnie says and pushes her plate away. "I don't want to eat this."

"Listen to your mother," James says.

Sally sends him a thankful look. For the most part, Winnie listens more to what her dear daddy says than her mother.

"But, Daddy. I don't want to."

"Eat your chicken," he says, gnawing at a thigh. "It's good."

"I don't like chicken," she says. "I don't want to eat birdies anymore."

"Now, I have never," Sally says.

James signals for her to calm down. Then takes over. "Why is that, Winnie, sweetie?"

"Because they're my friends. Like birdie. I don't want to eat my friends."

Sally rolls her eyes with a sigh. "Christ."

James tries another approach. "All right then, you don't have to eat the chicken. But eat your potatoes and your vegetables, all right?" He looks at Sally, who is about to protest, then says, "We can't really force her to hurt yet another bird, can we?"

Sally snorts. "I told you, I didn't mean to hurt it. I was just trying to get it off her shoulder and hopefully help it outside. That was all."

"You almost killed the birdie, Mommy," Winnie says, tears springing to her young eyes. "If it dies, I'll never forgive you. Never!"

Winnie gets up and storms out. They hear her door slam loudly a few seconds later.

6

Sally and James finish eating. She gets up from the table and does the dishes, while James goes to Winnie's room to talk to her, thinking she must be calmed down by now. He grabs the handle and knocks carefully while opening it slowly.

"Winnie, sweetie?"

He finds her sitting by the window, hovering over the shoebox. "Winnie, are you crying?"

He approaches her. She sniffles and looks up at him, then nods.

"What's wrong, sweetie?"

"Look at the birdie," she says.

He looks inside. The bird is still lying down on the cloth, motionless. "Is it breathing?" he asks.

She nods with a sniffle, then wipes her nose with the back of her hand. "Do you think she is going to die?"

He sighs. "I don't know, honey, but maybe we should prepare ourselves for the worst. Just in case."

Winnie sniffles again, then nods. "It's such a purdy birdie, don't you think, Daddy? Huh?"

He nods, even though he really doesn't think it is pretty. He has never thought of birds as pretty in any way. This one seems to have a beak way too big for its tiny head and he wonders whether it really can lift its head or not. Plus, it is white and kind of reminds him of an albino. He remembers reading about albino ravens that live in Canada and wonders if that is what it is.

But what is it doing all the way down here in Florida?

"It's a part of life, honey. You know that, right? That death is a natural part of life. Especially with animals. They don't live as long as we do. Their lives are filled with a lot more dangers than ours are."

She nods. "I know. Like moms with brooms."

He chuckles. "Well, yeah, that too. But also in nature."

The bird suddenly moves a wing.

"Look, Daddy," Winnie exclaims. "Did you see that?"

He nods. "I sure did. Maybe we shouldn't count him out just yet, huh?"

"I call him Zed. There's a boy in my class that I like. He's name is Zed."

"Zed," he says. "That's cute...I guess. But I thought you said the bird was a girl?"

"Does it matter? Zed can be a girl."

She puts her arms around her father's neck and pulls herself close to him. "What shall we do?"

"Tell you what. How about I tuck you in tonight—"

"Yay!"

"—and then we leave Zed here to recover from her— well, whatever it is she has—until tomorrow morning. If she is feeling better, then we'll set her free and let her fly away."

Winnie looks at him with big eyes. "And if she's not? What if she dies while I sleep, Daddy?"

"Then she wasn't supposed to survive. She can't get by in

nature if she's too weak anyway. If she's dead in the morning, we'll bury her in the backyard. Have a proper burial ceremony and sing a few songs for her. Say a proper goodbye."

Winnie nods and sniffles a few times, then holds her father tight. James enjoys being close to his daughter and smells her hair, thinking that sitting like this makes it all worth it. All the struggles at work. All the pressure. To know that he is giving her a perfect upbringing, a perfectly safe childhood with money enough, where the biggest care and concern is some stupid bird.

"Will you read from the birdie book to me before I go to sleep?" Winnie asks.

James nods and kisses her on the cheek. "Of course. Get ready for bed and then I'll be in and read to you."

S ally sneaks into Winnie's room, tiptoeing her way across the carpet, careful to not wake up her daughter. Winnie is sleeping heavily, snoring lightly under her covers, eyes closed. Sally walks to the shoebox, takes off the lid, and looks inside. She clasps her mouth, then puts the lid back on.

Still with the shoebox in her hand, she walks out of Winnie's room, into the hallway, where she takes another peek at the bird. It is still not moving.

Is it dead? It looks very dead.

Sally pokes it with her pointer finger, but the bird doesn't react. She pokes it again and again, and it doesn't move. She sighs.

Wonderful. Now I am going to have an inconsolable kid all morning. Just what I needed.

She rubs her forehead, wondering what to do. The bird is obviously dead. Is there any way she can avoid Winnie knowing that it has died? Maybe if she simply removes the box, the kid won't think of it when she wakes up? Maybe she'll simply have forgotten while she slept? It had happened often enough that she forgot stuff she had been upset about the next morning.

But not this. Not her birdie.

Sally exhales, then walks to the porch. She opens the lid again and looks at the darn bird. So many problems caused by this little feathered fellow.

How can such a small creature cause me so much trouble?

"Fly, birdie," she whispers. "Fly."

Of course, it doesn't, but it gives her an idea. What if it had actually flown? What would she tell Winnie? She could bury it here in the yard, and then tell Winnie the bird had simply flown off before she woke up? That she brought it outside to see if it was alive and then it took off?

I'll say I didn't know it would fly off. That I thought it was dead, but suddenly, it got better. Yeah, that'll work. It simply flew off to be with its friends. No, family. Family is better. Winnie loves family.

"That's it," Sally says and looks down at the bird. "You're going in the ground and no one will ever know."

Sally goes to the shed and finds a garden shovel. She digs a small hole, then reaches inside the box and picks the bird up. She looks at it one last time. Its head is slumped to the side, eyes closed. Sally almost feels sorry for it, till she remembers the feeling of the blackbird's claws as they were piercing through her scalp, and shivers. She hates birds. Boy, how she hates them.

"I am not regretting what I did, little birdie. You would have done the same to my daughter if I hadn't smacked you, wouldn't you? You were just waiting for your chance to get into her hair. To claw her scalp. I saw you looking at it, don't you for one second think I didn't see it."

Sally reaches down with the bird in her hand towards

the hole in the ground, when the bird suddenly opens its eyes and stares at her.

Sally shrieks and drops the bird. It unfolds its wings and soon it is in the air, flying, heading toward her. Sally screams as it comes closer, its beak pecking at her face.

"Get off me, you stupid bird," she screams and tries to hit it, but it keeps coming back, pecking at her face, ripping small chunks of skin out.

Sally screams again, then touches her face and has blood on her hands. The bird comes back at her and she manages to put her arm up to protect her face. The bird pecks at her arm and Sally screams in pain.

"Mom!"

Sally turns her head to see Winnie. She is standing behind her, hands at her sides, looking angrily at her mother, then at the hole in the ground.

"What do you think you're doing?"

"The bird was attacking me. I am telling you, look at my face!"

Winnie sighs as the bird recoils and sits on top of its box. Winnie walks towards it. Sally gasps and steps back.

"No. No. Don't. Stay away from that bird," she says. "Look at what it did to me. That bird is evil! Look how it hurt me."

But Winnie doesn't listen. She walks to the bird, reaches out her hand, and lets the bird jump up. Then she pets it gently on its head and the bird lets her. Sally is certain she's about to have a heart attack.

"Please, be careful. That bird attacked me, Winnie."

Her daughter looks at her. "Well, of course it did, what did you expect?" she asks. "First you knock it out with a broom and almost kill it, then you try to bury it while it's still alive?"

"She's got a point," James says, coming out from the house. "The bird probably isn't too fond of you right about now."

Sally snorts. "That bird is dangerous, Jim. Look at me. I'm bleeding."

James looks. "I admit it looks kind of bad. Maybe you should stay away from Zed from now on, huh?"

Winnie kisses the bird's beak. "You can stay in my room where the bad mommy won't be able to get to you."

"No. No. No," Sally says. "I am not having that bird inside of my house again. It belongs in nature, not in my house."

Winnie looks upset. "It's just woken up. It's still hurt, Mommy. It needs care. Look at it."

Sally does, then shakes her head. "It looks perfectly fine to me. Sure wasn't very sick when it attacked me."

James puts his arm around Sally. "Now, let's go and clean up your face and arm, and then Winnie can take Zed to her room where she won't disturb anyone, okay?"

"Jim, are you sure..."

"Sh. She's going to be fine. Look at how well she's handling it. It might be a good experience for her. Taking care of someone else besides herself. I'll help her. Don't worry. As soon as we're absolutely sure the bird is fine enough to get by on her own, we'll release her. You don't have to do anything. I'll take care of it all."

Sally exhales, not completely convinced that this will end well, but gives in. She nods. "All right, then. But I don't want to see that bird anywhere else in the house. It stays in her room, okay? And you keep it in that box whenever I enter the room. I don't want to have to fight it off again. That beak is sharp."

Sally looks at the pecking wounds on her arm. They're deep and nasty and she wrinkles her nose.

"I promise, Mommy," Winnie says, coming up to her, the bird on her arm.

Sally grunts as she looks at the bird. It's staring at her, it's green eyes fixated on her and it makes her shiver.

"I'm sure it'll be fine in a couple of days and then we'll get it out of your hair," James says, then laughs when realizing what he just said. "No pun intended."

"Ha. Ha. Very funny," Sally says and pulls away from them. "It's all just a joke to you, isn't it? Ha. Ha. Sally is afraid of birds, *hardehaha*."

Sally rushes toward the house, trying to get as far away from the bird as possible. She is walking with angry steps, grunting and grumbling along the way.

James yells after her. "I'm sorry. I didn't mean to upset you. I am sorry."

Sally finds no rest all day, knowing that bird is in there, in her daughter's room, while Winnie is at school and James is at work. She tries. She really tries to forget about it and go about her daily chores. She washes their clothes and strips her and James's bed of its sheets to wash them. She then walks to Winnie's room to get her bed sheets as well, but she stops on the other side of the door. Her hand on the handle, she decides it can wait. Winnie will have to have her sheets changed another day. There is no way she is going in there. Not today.

Sally grabs some meat out of the freezer and decides on beef today. No chicken for a few days. Then she grabs the vacuum cleaner and vacuums the house, avoiding Winnie's room till the end. She stands outside, looking at the door, wondering what would happen if she accidentally vacuumed the bird up, then lets the thought go again.

Winnie would never forgive you.

She decides she needs to grocery shop instead. Even though she could easily wait a few days. For once, she finds it kind of a relief to have to go shopping at Publix, to get out of the house. The thought of that bird flapping its wings frantically in there, pecking at the window, or the furniture, or whatever it might do, leaves her anxious.

What if it gets out somehow?

Sally lets go of the thought and leaves the house. In Publix, she manages to forget about it for a little while until she realizes James has written birdseed on the grocery list. Sally sighs.

Do I really have to feed it too? Pay money for food for it?

Sally sighs again, then picks up a bag of seeds, not knowing if it's the right one or even caring. She is sick of this bird and having to take care of it. Why can't it just fly back into nature and get lost?

Sally continues her shopping and buys an extra box of ice cream for herself. People are staring at her as she passes them pushing the cart. They're staring at her face. She has put Band-Aids on the wounds to make her look less horrifying, but that only makes her look like a teenager covering up her pimples.

She smiles at a lady who even stops to stare. Some people have no manners. Sally pushes her cart to the cashier and starts to put up her things. The guy packing her bags stares at her, and so does the lady behind the register. Sally tries to ignore them, even though she knows they're all wondering exactly what she is hiding behind all those Band-Aids.

Well, you'll never know, will you? You'll have to wonder about that till the day you die 'cause I ain't telling you.

She wonders for a second if people might think her husband is abusing her, but then lets the thought go. When the packer asks if he should help her to her car, she refuses. Mainly because she really doesn't need him to stare at her by the car too. Besides, she hates that long walk to the car when you don't know what to talk to the guy about.

Sally puts her groceries into the car and gets in. As she drives up to the gate leading to the island, she notices something on the top of the small house where the guard is sitting. A bird, very similar to the one at her house, only this one is bigger. She shakes her head as the gate opens, then drives past the small house. As she drives away, she looks in the rearview mirror and spots another bird, just like it, sitting next to the first one. Right when she takes a turn onto her own street, she notices three more of the same type of bird sitting on the wires above.

She parks the car in the driveway and hurries to get the groceries inside, staring anxiously at the birds, watching to see if they make a move. Finally, she's done and walks inside the house, closes the door behind her, then locks it, just to be sure.

When it is afternoon, Sally drives to the school to pick up her daughter. When they return, the birds are still there, sitting on the wires like they are waiting for them. And now there are even more of them, maybe twenty or so.

"Cool," Winnie says when she gets out of the car and spots them. "Maybe they're Zed's family. They sure look like her, don't you think, Mommy? Mommy? Are you okay, Mommy?"

"Let's go inside," Sally says and pulls her daughter's hand. She doesn't like the way the birds are staring at them with their glowing green eyes. She can't stop looking at their beaks that are twice or maybe three times the size of Zed's.

As soon as they enter the house, they are both overwhelmed by an excruciating noise.

"What is that?" Winnie asks.

Sally walks to the door of her daughter's room, then listens. She looks at Winnie and swallows hard.

"It's coming from your room. It sounds like...the bird... it's flapping around in there."

"Zed?" Winnie's face lights up.

"Oh, dear God. I can't stand that sound."

"She's better?" Winnie asks.

"I guess you could say that," Sally says. "Sure sounds like she is doing very well in there."

"Maybe she wants to go see her family? Maybe they have come to get her?" Winnie says, sounding very cheerful. "Do you think they can hear each other or even talk with one another?"

Sally doesn't quite share her enthusiasm. The sound of the bird flapping around frantically inside of the room terrifies her. Not to mention the thought of its twenty family members waiting outside, communicating or not.

"Get that thing out of my house," she says. "Get it OUT!"

"But, Mo-o-om," Winnie complains.

Sally shakes her head. "No. No. No more. This bird is going. I want it out of here. NOW."

Winnie sighs, annoyed. "Okay."

She walks to the door and puts her hand on the handle. She turns and looks at her mother.

"Are you sure I can't keep her? Just for a little while longer? I could get a cage? That way she wouldn't flap around at all."

Sally focuses hard on keeping her temper down. She closes her eyes for a few seconds, taking deep breaths, thinking of something nice, then opens them again. "I don't want to say this again, Winnie. Get the bird out of the house before I explode in a fit of rage."

Winnie grumbles. "Okay. Okay."

She opens the door and walks inside. "Hi, Zed. Hi, baby."

The fluttering sounds stop as soon as she closes the

door, and Sally calms down. She shakes her head and rolls her shoulders to relax them.

"In a few minutes, it'll all be over, Sally," she mumbles to herself. "In a few minutes, it's all over."

11

I t's too quiet. Sally is standing outside the door. She is listening, but can't hear a sound. What's going on in there? Did Winnie get the bird out?

Maybe she let it out the window.

Sally's heart is thumping in her throat as she waits. The silence scares her. The birds on the other side of the house are sitting eerily still on that wire. She watches them through the window, pulling the curtain aside. Not a movement. Not a sound. Nothing but staring green eyes.

Will they disappear if we get rid of the little one? Are they waiting for her? What are they anyway? I have never seen birds quite like these before.

Sally returns to her daughter's door and puts her ear to it. Silence. Nothing but terrifying silence.

"Winnie?" she asks and knocks lightly. "Is everything all right?"

There is no answer. Sally feels like she can't breathe. She knocks again, this time harder.

"Winnie? Is everything all right?"

Still, no answer. Not even a sound.

"Winnie?"

Sally breathes heavily as she puts her hand on the door handle. She finds it hard to catch her breath. The thought of facing that bird again makes her hyperventilate.

Calm down, Sally. I am sure everything is all right. I am sure Winnie is just fine in there.

She lets go of the handle and looks at her hand, realizing she can't do it. She can't go in there. She's too scared of a darn little bird.

And that is when she hears it. The piercing screams of her daughter's cry for help, followed by:

"MOOOOOOM!"

"Winnie!"

Sally pulls the handle, opens the door, and slams it up against the wall behind it. Inside, she spots her daughter, sitting in the corner, both of her hands covering her face. The bird is above her, hovering above her, pecking at her face, getting in between her arms to find the bare skin, then pecking, ripping it to blood, using its claws too.

"MOOOOM. Mommy. Mommy!"

Sally stares at the bird, then at her daughter. She looks around for something to use. She grabs the lightsaber Winnie got for her birthday from her cousin, who thought Winnie had to be just as fond of the *Star Wars* movies as he is. The bird is in the air, now diving down towards Winnie, claws first. Sally swings the plastic sword through the air and hits the bird just as it is about to attack her daughter once again.

The bird squeaks, then flies through the air, hitting the window with a thud. The bird lands on the carpet. Completely out of it, Sally rushes to it and sees that it is still moving. She lifts the sword once again and slams it down on the bird, and then again and again, till blood comes out of it and it lies completely still.

"Mommy?"

Sally turns to face her daughter, removing hair from her face. Winnie looks at her, her face ripped and bleeding.

"Mommy? Is it gone now?"

"Zed's dead, baby. Zed's dead."

12

J ames is in a meeting when he receives the call. His secretary peeks inside the meeting room and tells him it is urgent. Soon after, he is rushing through town to get to Arnold Palmer Children's Hospital in Orlando, where Winnie has been transferred.

He finds Sally sitting by Winnie's bedside in her room. Winnie smiles when she sees her father.

"Daddy!"

"Winnie, baby," he exclaims and rushes to her bed. He looks at her face, then feels a huge lump in his stomach. "Are you all right?" He looks at Sally. "Is she all right? What do the doctors say?"

Sally nods. "She'll be okay. Wounds are pretty deep, though. They'll leave scars."

James clasps his mouth while tears well into his eyes, as he looks at her face and arms. "And that bird did this to you? That sweet little birdie? Oh, dear God, you poor, poor thing."

"Yeah, well, it's a little late for all that now," Sally says.

James looks at her. "What's that supposed to mean?"

Sally shakes her head and looks away. "Nothing."

"What? You're blaming me?"

"Well..." Sally gives him a look.

"Because I let her keep the bird. How was I supposed to know it would do...this?" he asks.

Sally sighs, then corrects Winnie's pillow behind her head. "Mo-om," her daughter complains.

"It's not like I didn't tell you," Sally says and points at her own face.

James blushes. He feels terrible, even worse than when he just came in the room. She's right, isn't she? He did know. He saw her face, yet he still allowed the bird back into the house. What kind of husband is he? What kind of father?

"I...I am...I feel terrible," he says.

"It's okay, Daddy," Winnie says. "It's not your fault. It was that stupid birdie's fault."

Sally smiles, then puts a hand on his shoulder. "There really isn't much we can do about it now, is there?"

He looks into her eyes. Her eyes are filled with love for him and forgiveness, but he can't forgive himself, not after what has happened, after what he did to her, to his beloved daughter. Anger wells up inside of him.

"I am gonna kill that bird..."

"Mom already did," Winnie says.

"What?"

"Mommy killed the birdie," Winnie repeats. "Smashed it against the window using my lightsaber. You should have seen it, Daddy, it was awesome. Left a huge stain of blood on the window and everything. Then, when it fell to the floor, she hit it again and again till it was completely dead. It was awesome, Daddy. Mom saved me. Like a Jedi."

James sighs and puts an arm around his wife's shoulder.

He looks into her eyes with a gentle exhale. "I guess she is our little hero, then. And I guess it is all over? No more birds in the house?"

Sally nods confidently. "The bird won't bother us ever again, that's for sure. It's over."

Winnie is discharged from the hospital late in the afternoon. Sally and James are told to keep the wounds very clean and to not let Winnie go in the pool for a few weeks. She is given a bag of painkillers along with a bottle of liquid morphine in case it gets really bad, and asked to go see her own physician in two days to check on the wounds and make sure they're not infected and that they're healing properly. Sally is also handed a pamphlet for a plastic surgeon who can repair the scars when Winnie grows older.

James sighs happily in the car on the way home.

"What?" Sally asks.

"I'm just...so grateful. It could have been so much worse." He looks at Winnie in the rearview mirror and smiles as their eyes meet.

"You don't think it was bad enough?" Sally asks.

"Of course I do. It was terrible, but think of how much worse it could have been. What if it had pecked her in the... in the..." he leans over and whispers the last part, "eyes?"

Sally nods. He has a point. The bird could easily have

blinded her in at least one of her eyes. The thought is terrifying and Sally doesn't want to think it to the end. It's bad enough that her daughter will grow up with scars on her face because no one would listen to her when she told them that bird was dangerous. Even though the evidence was pretty clear when looking at what it did to her. Very clear, indeed.

Don't start again, Sally. You promised yourself to forgive him, remember? You promised. It's the only way to move on after this. Don't get all agitated again. He made a mistake. Forgive him.

But it is easier said than done. Sally can't escape the thought that if only they had listened, if only she had been more determined, if only she had stood her ground and not given in, this would never have happened. But, oh, no, the bird was harmless. It was just her.

Yeah, right!

Sally blows raspberries in the car without noticing it. She looks embarrassed at James when he gives her a stare.

"What's that, dear?"

She shakes her head. "Nothing. I was just lost in my thoughts."

He looks at her like he doesn't really believe her. She shrugs with an awkward smile. "Can't wait to get home."

"Me either," he says. He looks in the mirror at Winnie in the back. "How are we doing back there?"

"I'm tired, Daddy," Winnie says.

Sally turns and looks at her. She looks horrible. Forty-eight stitches in total, the doctor told them. Sally feels her own face and is grateful that at least the bird didn't dig as deep into her skin as it did to her daughter, even though she would trade places with her any day, if only she could. The doctor had been joking with her, asking her if she liked pirates because she was going to look just like a real pirate after this. With all those scars. Sally wasn't so sure pirates had that many scars. Winnie thought it was cool, luckily, but she probably wasn't going to once she got a little older. If only the other kids wouldn't pick on her. That is one of Sally's great concerns. Not only is Winnie quite overweight, at least she used to have a pretty face. Now that is gone.

James drives up to the gate and the guard greets him, then opens the gate. They drive onto the island, turn right onto their street, then drive into the driveway. It is dark when they get out of the car and start to walk up to the house.

James puts the key in the keyhole when a sound suddenly makes them all turn around.

14

Hundreds of birds are staring back at them. White ravens with green eyes, sitting on the wires, on the rooftops, in the bushes. One lets out a loud cawing sound and they all respond in unison.

"KR-AAA, KR-AAA, KR-A-A-A. KR-AAA, KR-AAA, KR-A-A-A. KR-AAA, KR-AAA, KR-A- A-A."

Sally grabs Winnie and pulls her close. "W-w-what is this? What's going on here, James?"

James shakes his head. "I-I-I don't know."

Winnie lets out a loud whimper. The birds look a lot like Zed, but they're bigger, a lot bigger. One rises above them into the air and shows a wingspan of about eight feet. It is hovering above them, making loud noises, like it is commanding its soldiers, telling them what to do.

"I...think we better get inside," James says and returns to the keys that are still stuck in the door.

"Hurry, hurry," Sally says, listening to the keys jangle as James frantically tries to unlock the door.

"Damn lock," he grumbles.

"Hurry, Jim. It's getting closer. And it's getting the others to follow it, now hurry, will you, Jim, please?"

"I'm doing the best I can. The door won't unlock."

"James, please. Hurry."

Just as he hears the sweet song of the lock being opened, one bird dives towards them, grabs Sally's hair with its claws, and pulls forcefully, pulling out a huge lock of hair.

Sally is screaming as more birds dive towards them, surrounding them, flapping their wings, getting tangled in their hair, pecking at their scalps and faces. They're all screaming, trying to fight the birds off. Sally manages to get two away from her face, then grabs Winnie and pulls her towards the door. A bird is tangled in her hair and can't get loose. The girl is screaming, panicking.

"Mommy, Mommy, MOMMY!"

Sally grabs the bird's wing and pulls. "Mommy, you're hurting me, you're hurting me!"

The bird is screaming at her, at least that's what it sounds like, pecking at her fingers while she is pulling its wing. It is flapping crazily when she pulls forcefully again and manages to get it out of her daughter's hair.

"My eye! My eye!" James's screams are piercing through Sally's bones. "It pecked me in the eye."

Sally looks at him and sees blood running from his eye, then screams. "James. Get inside!!"

The bird keeps pecking at his face, but he manages to slap it off, then stumbles backward into the hallway. Sally grabs Winnie by the arm as more birds surround them, making it impossible to see or move. Sally yells at them, trying to scare them away while holding her daughter in her arms and dragging her towards the door. She is screaming and yelling at the birds, slapping them as they come at her. But she can hardly move. Too many birds, beaks, and fluttering wings make it hard for her to get to the door, and soon she curls herself around her girl to protect her from the attacks. That's when James comes out of the house, still bleeding from his eye, holding an umbrella between his hands and starts to knock the birds off her. He then grabs both her and Winnie and pulls them inside, then kicks the door to slam it shut. The sound of birds hitting against the door is deafening.

15

"James! Your eye!"

Sally stares at James while the birds keep flying against the door and windows. A rain of birds is slamming against the house, every thud and bump causing Sally to jump in fear.

"I think...I think..." James says.

"The blood," Sally says. "We need to get you to the hospital."

She grabs her cellphone and dials 911.

"Yes, hello? I need an ambulance, fast. My husband is hurt. We're on Lansing Island. Birds...birds pecked him in the eye. I fear he might lose the eye, please come fast, please!"

"Ma'am, I need you to calm down a little bit. We are currently trying to get to the island since we are receiving a massive amount of calls from citizens who have been attacked and hurt by birds and birds slamming against their houses. We will try and get to you as soon as possible. Now, what number are you in?"

"433."

"Okay, ma'am. Now, I need you to stay calm. As I said, we're trying to get out there, but right now we can't even enter the island. We will get to your husband as soon as we can."

"You can't get here? But...but...he's gonna lose his eye!"

"I am sorry, ma'am. We're trying as hard as we can. I need you to stay calm."

Sally hangs up, grabs her purse, and hands James Winnie's morphine. He drinks from the bottle, gulping it down greedily, while Sally finds the remote and turns the TV on. Shots of her beloved island taken from a helicopter greet her like a slap in the face.

"That's our island!" Winnie exclaims. "Mommy? What's happening to our island? Why is our island on TV?"

"Sh. I need to hear this," Sally says, her heart in her throat. "They say no one can get to the island. The birds are attacking people and the ambulances all over the place, crashing the windows, flocking around the cars as they try to drive through. They're gonna try to helicopter the paramedics in. Look."

James comes up behind her and they watch together. James lights a cigarette. Sally gives him a look. He gives her one back, stating *Really? You wanna focus on that now?*

The news helicopter stays up high as the paramedics are trying to be lowered in by the chopper trying to land on the island.

"Look at the birds!" James says, watching everything with his hand over the bleeding eye, forgetting for a few seconds that he is torn in excruciating pain. "Are they attacking the chopper?"

"It looks like it," Sally says.

"Look, the windshield just cracked."

"That flock of birds flew into the propeller. It's going

sideways now. It's gonna crash. Oh, dear God, Jim, it's going to crash on our island."

They look at each other just as the television crew screams and it is followed by a loud crash, coming from not far away. Winnie throws herself into Sally's arms as they are pushed to the carpet. The entire house is shaking.

"Dear God," Sally exclaims and looks at the TV screen, where nothing but smoke is seen on the camera. As the smoke clears a little, she can see the flames from the burning chopper that landed on top of the Richardson's house, three houses down from Sally and James. Luckily, they told Sally they were visiting their newborn grandson in Denver this week.

"We need to get off the island," James says. "Before that fire spreads."

16

"We can't go out there," Sally says. She is standing by the door leading to the yard. Bird after bird is slamming against the window in a constant flow.

"They'll kill us."

James comes up next to her. He pops the top of Winnie's morphine bottle again and Sally wonders how much he has had. She knows he is in a lot of pain; the eye is nothing but nerves, but still. How much can he take and still think straight?

"It's our only chance, Sally," he says. His speech is getting slurred.

Can she trust his judgment?

He clears his throat. She looks at Winnie, who is sitting in the middle of the living room, in a fetal position, arms covering her head and crying.

"The fire will spread fast in this wind," James says.

Sally swallows hard and looks at the window. Birds keep slamming against it like big hail. Blood is smeared on the outside and white feathers are stuck in it. Sally can still feel the beak from the small bird as it pecked her face. These birds are even bigger, maybe twice or three times the size.

"I...I don't know if I can do it," she says.

Barely has she finished the sentence when a loud thud, followed by frantic flapping, breaks the silence in the living room as a bird finds its way down the chimney. Winnie looks up, sees the white bird flapping around, then screams.

"BIR-DIIII-EEEE!"

Sally jumps for the umbrella that James has left on the carpet and hurries towards it as it gets ready to attack Winnie. It dives towards the child, grabs her hair, and pulls it forcefully, Winnie screaming even louder.

"MO-M-M-Y-YYY!!!!"

Sally swings the umbrella through the air and hits the bird so it slams against the chimney with a loud noise. The bird falls to the ground, flaps its wings a few times, again and again trying to get up, but not succeeding. Sally pants and stares at it, then walks to it, lifts the umbrella high in the air and lets it fall on it over and over again, as hard as possible.

"It's dead, Mommy, it's dead!" Winnie screams.

Still, Sally doesn't stop. She keeps hitting the bird till they can hardly tell it is a bird anymore. Still, she keeps going and going at it. James finally puts his hand on her shoulder.

"It's dead, Sally."

She stops. Panting, she looks up at him, blowing a lock of hair away from her face. "I just needed this."

"What we need is to get out of here. The fire is at our neighbor's house now," he says. "It's licking the side of ours. Soon, it will get ahold of our roof, and then it's over. The wind is not helping. We have to get out of here. Now."

Sally pauses and looks into the road. She sees old Mr.

Monty running down the street. At least she thinks it is him inside the flock of birds. He screams and tries to fight the birds off with his cane, but once he hits one, more just come back at him. Finally, he is forced to his knees. Sally feels terrible just watching him like this. She hates feeling so helpless.

James disappears, then returns holding his rifle that he uses for duck hunting. He cocks it and looks at Sally with the eyes of a madman.

"Fasten your seatbelts, my dear. It's going to be a bumpy ride."

17

Armed with an umbrella each, Sally and Winnie follow James to the French doors leading to the yard. Birds are still coming at the house in a massive amount and James can't help but wonder where all these birds are coming from all of a sudden and what the heck has gotten into them, attacking them like this, attacking the entire island?

Could it be just because we killed that little bird? Because Sally killed it?

The thought lingers for a few seconds before James kicks open the French doors. While yelling, he starts to shoot. The hope is that the sound of the shots will scare the birds away. It usually does when he goes duck hunting. Just one shot will make all the birds in the area take off at once, even from treetops far away.

A bird comes at him and he shoots it. It is hit and falls to the ground. But before he can reload, tens of his friends are back, flocking around James, pulling his hair, pecking at his face and bare arms. Behind him, Sally and Winnie are fighting the birds off using the umbrellas, but not having much success, judging from their screams.

"Get the hell out of here!!!" James screams, then fires yet another shot. As usual, he doesn't miss. The bird falls to the ground, dead as a...well, bird, but it's not enough. As soon as one goes down, ten or maybe even twenty of his friends take over. James soon turns to try and wipe them away, swinging the rifle through the air, hitting a few birds, but not getting rid of them. Behind him, Winnie and Sally are screaming loudly.

Why aren't they afraid? Why didn't the sound scare them? What the heck is wrong with these darn birds?

"JIM!" Sally screams. "We have to get back inside!!"

They pull back. A bird is on top of James's head as he rushes for the French doors. It is pecking his scalp, piercing its beak deep into his head. It hurts like crazy and James is screaming.

Sally sees it, swings her umbrella, and hits it. The bird doesn't even move. It just takes the blow, then continues to peck, like it is drilling into his brain.

PECK-PECK-PECK

"Get it off me, get it off!" James is yelling as they storm in through the doors, dropping the rifle to the floor. Sally closes the doors behind them, barely keeping the massive amount of birds out. Winnie falls to the ground, crying, bleeding from her face and arms.

James is getting hysterical. Panic erupting inside of him as he tries to reach up and grab the bird.

"Get it off!"

Sally swings the umbrella again and again, but the bird doesn't move. It's like it doesn't even feel the pain.

"I can't get it off, Jim. I can't get it off. It won't let go, no matter how much I hit. Or how hard."

"It hurts," he screams and falls to his knees. "Please, help me."

"Daddy!" Winnie shrieks. "Help Daddy!"

"I'm trying to. I'm trying my best here," Sally yells through gritted teeth while hitting the bird over and over again. "I don't know what to do. I don't know how to get it off him."

"Just do something. Anything," James yells desperately.

Sally looks around her, then heads for the fireplace where she picks up the fire poker. With a loud yell—worthy of an Amazon warrior—she runs towards James, who is still kneeling. James sees the look on his wife's face, then screams as he sees the fire poker come closer. He can't see what is happening, but hears a plump sound and feels the extreme relief when the claws lets go of his scalp.

James looks up and sees Sally standing with the fire poker in her hand, still pierced through the bird sitting at the other end like it is ready to be barbecued.

"Yay, Mommy, you got it!" Winnie exclaims. "You got it."

18

Panting with exhaustion and in deep pain, they rest on the carpet for a few seconds. James is looking at his wife with the dead bird still in her hand.

"Thanks, babe," he says.

"No problem," she says and pulls the bird off the fire poker before she puts it on the ground. She looks at the window. "But even though we got rid of one, there are still so many of them out there. It's like, the more we kill, the more return."

James chuckles, not because he is amused, more because of the bizarreness of the entire situation, the powerlessness.

"Yeah, they're like weeds. We can't get rid of them."

Sally's face lights up. "What did you say?"

"We can't get rid of them?"

"No, the other part."

"They're like weeds?"

She looks at him with a look he doesn't remember ever seeing in his wife's eyes before. Meanwhile, a loud sound comes from the French doors. James turns to look and sees the birds. It is like they're trying to penetrate the doors.

Some are pecking on the windows and soon the glass cracks.

"Mommy?" Winnie says.

But Mommy isn't there. James turns his head to look for her, but she is no longer in the living room.

"Where'd she go?" he asks.

Winnie shrugs then returns to watching the birds outside the closed doors. "I think they're trying to get in," she says.

"That's silly," James says, chuckling again, but it comes out awkwardly. "They can't come in here."

And just as he finishes the sentence, a beak pecks through the glass. Winnie screams again. James gasps. The bird's beak seems to be stuck for a little while before it finally manages to pull it out, just to return to pecking and shattering the glass. Soon after, it jumps inside, tilts its head to one side, then to the other, like it is studying them, sizing up its victims.

"Winnie. I need you to sit completely still," James says. "Maybe it won't see you if you do."

Winnie whimpers and hides her face in her knees. James looks for the fire poker, then leans over and grabs it nice and quietly, careful to not attract the bird's attention. He picks it up but makes a noise in pain. The bird lifts off the carpet and soars into the air with what sounds mostly like a loud scream.

KR-A. KR-AA. KR-AAA.

It sounds almost like it is calling for its friends. The bird sits on the black IKEA curtain rod that Sally likes so much. Seconds later, another bird finds its way through the hole in the glass and joins the first one. James is holding on tight to the fire poker when a third bird comes through, then a fourth, and soon there is an entire flock of them sitting above the door, waiting.

James has a hard time holding the fire poker still in his hand. He looks at Winnie and imagines what he is going to do once they make their move. There is more pecking behind them and soon another beak finds its way through the glass, then another and another. Birds are crawling inside one after the other, while others are putting so much pressure on the French doors, they soon cave and slam open, the doors falling off their hinges, letting in thousands of white fluttering birds.

19

"They're coming, Daddy. They're coming!"

Winnie shrieks and pulls back. The birds have gathered in one big crowd. It's like they're waiting, getting ready to attack. James comes up behind Winnie, grabs her by the waist, holding out the fire poker, ready to protect her. He can't hold it still. His hands are shaking too massively. A bird makes a move and he turns to face it, pointing the poker at it.

"Don't you dare come near my daughter," he hisses. "I will pierce this thing right through you."

He talks to them like they understand him. He wants to let them know he isn't afraid of them, even though he is terrified. He knows perfectly well he doesn't stand a chance. He knows he can only kill one of them with the fire poker. Only one. After that, he'll be left unarmed and helpless. He wonders if the birds know it too. Are they that intelligent?

The massive flock of birds soon surrounds them and James is swinging the fire poker back and forth, hitting a few —missing many.

"Get away from us, you flying rats," he yells as they dive

towards them. Some have their claws first, others their beaks. He sees one with his only eye, diving towards him, then swings the poker, but misses and it goes directly for his eye, the only one he has left. James screams loudly, thinking he is going to lose the other eye, when he suddenly hears a hissing sound coming from behind him. Not a hiss like a cat would make it. No, this is different. He knows this sound very well from weekends spent working in the yard.

James pushes Winnie to the ground and jumps on top of her as the flames shoot above his head and hit the birds. His head on the carpet, he watches as the birds drop to the ground by the tens. The smell of burnt feathers would normally make him feel sick, but not today. Today it fills him with the sweet sense of victory. Seeing bird after bird drop makes him so thrilled he feels like laughing.

Hundreds of birds die, and soon the rest realize what is going on, then turn around and flee. The living room is soon empty of birds, well of the living ones; the floor is still packed with the dead ones. The curtains are on fire and so is Sally's beloved couch, but the birds are gone. No more fluttering, no more kra-ing, no more pecking.

James lifts his head and looks up to see Sally standing there, the flame-throwing weed killer in her hand.

"Of course," he says, laughing as he gets up. There still isn't anything funny about the situation, but the relief makes him want to laugh.

Sally smiles. "You okay?"

"Think so." He helps Winnie up as well. She is still crying. He picks her up and lets her cry on his shoulder. "How did you...?"

Sally shrugs with a grin. "I guess desperate times *do* call for desperate measures, like they say."

He smiles and nods.

"They sure do."

Sally walks to the opening leading to the yard, where the French doors were before they caved in. She steps outside and fires the weed killer again, probably to scare away the birds. She hits a bunch and they drop like flies. It's the sweetest sound in the world. The rest of the birds flee. Sally then turns and looks at James.

"Follow me. These birds are going down."

He has never felt more attracted to her.

20

They run for the boat. Sally makes sure no birds come close to any of them, killing each and every bird that does, frying it till it falls out of the dark sky, and enjoying every second of it. On the dock, they get into their speedboat and, minutes later, they take off, James steering the boat into the darkness of the Intracoastal waters.

Sally is shooting fire in all directions, and soon the birds seem to leave them alone. The further they get from the island, the less they try to attack them.

Soon, Sally doesn't even have to shoot anymore. With a deep sigh, she looks at the island, her beloved home. From where she is standing on the back of the boat, it looks like a war zone.

"Our island is burning," she says.

"All the pretty houses," Winnie says and comes up next to her.

"Hey, you said pretty," Sally says and smiles. She already misses how she used to say it. Kids grow up so fast.

Winnie leans against her mother's hip and holds her tight. Sally feels relieved. She sits down on the boat and grabs Winnie in her lap. They sit like that, watching the burning island, getting further and further away from it when suddenly another boat approaches them.

"It's the Coast Guard," James says and slows down the boat.

The Coast Guard boat comes up on the side of them. A man pokes his head out, takes one look at James's wounds, then says, "Are you all right, sir?"

"I think we will be," he says.

"Let us take you to the hospital, sir. You're hurt. Someone needs to look at that eye, sir."

James sighs deeply. He has almost forgotten how hurt he is, but now the pain is back and he is out of morphine. They throw an anchor to keep the speedboat there till they can get out there and pick it up. They board the Coast Guard vessel and head towards land, going a lot faster than in their small speedboat.

"Darn birds," the man from the Coast Guard says.

"Where did they come from all of a sudden?" James asks. "All these birds?"

The man looks at him, then shakes his head. "No one knows. But they found a nest. In the mangroves, not far from the island. Thousands of eggs they said. They have been hiding in those darn mangroves for a very long time. No one ever gets near them since they're not allowed to, due to them being endangered and all. You know, you can't even go near them."

"Oh, dear God," Sally says.

"Had to kill them all. That's what I heard. The Air Force came in those big choppers and had to drop a bomb. Can you believe it? A bomb to get rid of some birds. That's some crazy sh…"

The man restrains himself when he sees Sally react to

his attempt at cursing. He looks at Winnie, then lifts his cap. "Sorry, ma'am."

"It's all right," she says. "I think we can all agree we have seen some crazy sh...shtuff tonight."

"Sure have, ma'am. Sure have."

"So, you're telling me they have destroyed all the eggs where the birds were coming from?" James asks.

"Each and every one of them," he says. "There will be no more birds as soon as they have killed the last live ones. Won't be long, though, and then it'll be all over, sir. It'll all be over soon."

"That's a relief," James says and grabs his wife's hand in his. "That sure is a relief."

SIX WEEKS LATER.

SOMEWHERE IN CENTRAL FLORIDA.

21

Andy was sent home from school, again. He is used to it. It's no big deal, really. Besides, it was all worth it. Putting the dead roach on top of Rhianna's hair during art-class was the best prank he had come up with in a long time.

Boy, that girl could scream.

Andy chuckles as he thinks about it, running in the yard leading towards the lake. He crawls under the fence, even though his mother has strictly told him to stay near the house, where she can keep an eye on him. His dog, Lusk, is with him. Andy has a ball in his hand that he throws for the dog to fetch. They run towards the lake. Andy is wearing his trunks. He wants to go swimming, even though his mother has told him to never go into that murky water again. Not since there was a gator spotted down there last month. But Andy ain't afraid of no gator. No, sirree.

They say he might be gifted. Andy heard them talk about it the last time he was in the principal's office. Not today...today he was just sent home since the principal was out of town. But earlier. They even had this doctor come talk to him and give him all these sheets with riddles and pictures for him to solve. It wasn't very hard. They say that's why he doesn't behave well in school. He isn't challenged enough. Andy thinks it's awesome that they would think that and laughs again at the idea of him joining a program for gifted children. As long as it gets him out of class every now and then, he's down with it. Any of it.

"Wait for me, Lusk," he yells as the dog runs ahead of him. Andy speeds up and runs as fast as he can without tripping. He loves the feeling of his heart pounding like it's about to jump out of his chest. It's fun.

The path leads him through a small forest, and soon he can spot the mangroves in the distance that mark the beginning of the lake.

"They hide in the mangroves," he can hear his mother say. "'em alligators. That's where they hide."

Andy laughs loudly, then slows down as he approaches the water. The thought that there might be a gator or maybe more than one, thrills Andy. He always wanted to go gator hunting with his dad, like some of the other kids from his school do. But his father isn't a hunter. He works from home, doing programming on his computer, getting paler by the day. It's boring.

"At least take me fishing?" Andy had pleaded with him earlier in the week.

"I don't fish," he had answered, not even bothering to look up from his screen. "Never have, never will."

"Besides, it's a bad idea going down to that lake anyway," his mother had taken over. "Never know what is down there."

But Andy knows exactly what is down there, that is why he is in such a hurry. He wants to see the gator before it disappears. For so many days, he wondered if it was still there, ever since the choleric Mrs. Peterson said she had seen it. She had seen its eyes lurking at her, wanting to grab a bite of her meaty thighs (that's how she put it while snapping her fat fingers in the air while talking to Andy's mother). There was a girl not far from there who had been bitten by a gator some months ago but had escaped by poking two fingers into its nostrils. Andy knows he would do the same, and part of him really wants to try it. Today is the day because he is already in so much trouble it doesn't matter if there is one more thing. Andy is clever that way. Maybe that is why they keep calling him *gifted*.

"Wait for me, Lusk," he yells again and rushes to keep up with the dog. The dog suddenly stops and drops the ball. Andy catches up with him. Lusk barks.

"What's the matter, Lusk?" Andy says, feeling excited. "Is there something behind those bushes?"

The dog keeps barking, then backs up. Something is definitely scaring it. It whimpers now, then suddenly takes off.

"Hey, Lusk. Come back here!" But the dog keeps running, not even looking back. "Stupid dog," he says, then looks at the tall mangrove in front of him, wondering what exactly it is that has scared Lusk so much. Could it be the alligator? Could he be that lucky?

Can't hurt to take a look.

Andy approaches the bushes, then pulls them aside, creating a path for him to get through. As he approaches the water, he suddenly stops, his jaw literally dropping. In front of him, there is no water, no lake. Well, the lake and water are probably there, but he can't see it. The entire lake is covered in nests floating on top of the water. Huge nests with hundreds of thousands of eggs. In some nests, he spots small baby birds, their mouths open, ready to be fed, while thousands of mother birds hover above them.

Big white birds with sparkling green eyes.

AFTERWORD

Dear Reader,

Thank you for purchasing The Bird. I hope you had fun reading it. I sure had fun writing it. Boy, birds can be scary, right? I always thought they were. I hate it when one accidentally gets into the house and flaps around like crazy. I know a lot of people share this fear. I simply had to write about it.

Since it is a short story, there really isn't much to tell about it, except that Lansing Island does exist and so do white ravens. They usually live up north in Canada and are very rare, and they usually don't have green eyes. I don't think they attack people either, but you never know, do you?

Don't forget to leave a review if you can.

Thank you,

Willow

BOOKS BY THE AUTHOR

MYSTERY/HORROR NOVELS

- In One Fell Swoop
- Umbrella Man
- Blackbird Fly
- To Hell in a Handbasket
- Edwina

7TH STREET CREW SERIES

- What Hurts the Most
- You Can Run
- You Can't Hide
- Careful Little Eyes

EMMA FROST SERIES

- Itsy Bitsy Spider
- Miss Dolly had a Dolly
- Run, Run as Fast as You Can
- Cross Your Heart and Hope to Die
- Peek-a-Boo I See You
- Tweedledum and Tweedledee
- Easy as One, Two, Three

- There's No Place like Home
- Slenderman
- Where the Wild Roses Grow

JACK RYDER SERIES

- Hit the Road Jack
- Slip out the Back Jack
- The House that Jack Built
- Black Jack

REBEKKA FRANCK SERIES

- One, Two...He is Coming for You
- Three, Four...Better Lock Your Door
- Five, Six...Grab your Crucifix
- Seven, Eight...Gonna Stay up Late
- Nine, Ten...Never Sleep Again
- Eleven, Twelve...Dig and Delve
- Thirteen, Fourteen...Little Boy Unseen

HORROR SHORT-STORIES

- Better watch out
- Eenie, Meenie
- Rock-a-Bye Baby
- Nibble, Nibble, Crunch

- Humpty Dumpty
- Chain Letter
- Mommy Dearest
- The Bird

PARANORMAL SUSPENSE/FANTASY NOVELS

AFTERLIFE SERIES

- Beyond
- Serenity
- Endurance
- Courageous

THE WOLFBOY CHRONICLES

- A Gypsy Song
- I am WOLF

DAUGHTERS OF THE JAGUAR

- Savage
- Broken

ABOUT THE AUTHOR

 The Queen of Scream, Willow Rose, is an international best-selling author. She writes Mystery/Suspense/Horror, Paranormal Romance and Fantasy. She is inspired by authors like James Patterson, Agatha Christie, Stephen King, Anne Rice, and Isabel Allende. She lives on Florida's Space Coast with her husband and two daughters. When she is not writing or reading, you'll find her surfing and watching the dolphins play in the waves of the Atlantic Ocean. She has sold more than two million books.

Connect with Willow online:

willow-rose.net
madamewillowrose@gmail.com

HIT THE ROAD JACK

EXCERPT

For a special sneak peak of Willow Rose's Bestselling Mystery Novel *Hit the Road Jack* (JACK RYDER #1) turn to the next page.

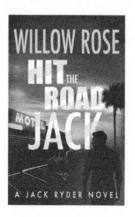

~

This could be Heaven or this could be Hell
~ Eagles, Hotel California 1977

~

PART I

DON'T COME BACK
NO MORE

1

MAY 2012

She has no idea who she is or where she is and cares to know neither. For some time, for what seems like forever, she has been in this daze. This haze, in complete darkness with nothing but the sounds. Sounds coming from outside her body, from outside her head. Sometimes, the sounds fade and there is only the darkness.

As time passes, she becomes aware that there are two realities. The one in her mind, filled with darkness and pain and then the one outside of her, where something or someone else is living, acting, smelling and...singing.

Yes, that's it. Someone is singing. Does she know the song?

...What you say?

The darkness is soon replaced by light. Still, her eyes are too heavy to open. Her consciousness returns slowly. Enough to start asking questions. Where is she? How did she end up here? A series of pictures of her at home come to her mind. She is waiting. What is she waiting for?

...I guess if you said so.

Him. She is waiting for him. She is checking her hair in

the mirror every five minutes or so. Then correcting the make-up, looking at the clock again. Where is he? She looks out through the window and at the street and the many staring neighboring windows. A feeling of guilt hits her. Somehow, it seems wrong for this kind of thing to take place in broad daylight.

...That's right!

A car drives up. The anticipation. The butterflies in her stomach. The sound of the doorbell. She is straightening her dress and taking a last glance in the mirror. The next second, she is in his embrace. He is holding her so tight she closes her eyes and breathes him in until his lips cover hers and she swims away.

...Whoa, Woman, oh woman, don't treat me so mean.

His breath is pumping against her skin. She feels his hands on her breasts, under her skirt, coming closer, while he presses her up against the wall. She feels him in his hand. He is hard now, moaning in her ear.

"Where's your husband?" he whispers.

"Work," she moans back, feeling self-conscious. Why did he have to bring up her husband? The guilt is killing her. "The kids are in school."

"Good," he moans. "No one can ever know. Remember that. No one."

...You're the meanest old woman that I've ever seen.

He pushes himself inside of her and pumps. She lets herself get into the moment, but as soon as it is over, she finds herself regretting it...while he zips up the pants of his suit and kisses her gently on the lips, whispering, *same time next week?* She regrets having started it all. They are both married with children, and this is only an affair. Could never be anything else, even if she dreamt about it. The sex is great, but she wants more than just seeing him on her lunch break. But she can never tell him. She can never explain to him how much she hates this awkward moment that follows the sex.

"They're expecting me at the office...I have a meeting," he says, and puts his tie back on. "I'd better..."

...Hit the road, Jack!

She finally opens her eyes with a loud gasp. The bright light hurts her. Water is being splashed in her face. She can't breathe. The bathtub is slippery when she tries to get up. Her eyes lock with another set of eyes. The eyes of a man. He is staring at her with a twisted smile. She gasps again, suddenly remembering those dark chili eyes.

"*I guess if you said so...I'd have to pack my things and go,*" he sings.

"You," she gasps. Breathing is hard for her. She feels like she is still choking. She is hyperventilating. Panicking.

The man smiles. On his neck crawls a snake. How does that old saying go again? *Red, black, yellow kills a fellow?* This one is all of that, all those colors. It stares at her while moving its tongue back and forth. The man is holding a washcloth in his hand. She looks down at her naked body. The smell of chlorine is strong and makes her eyes water.

"You tried to kill me," she says, while panting with anxiety.

I have to get home. Help me. I have to get home to my children! Oh, God. I can hear their voices! Am I going mad? I think I can hear them!

"I guess I didn't do a very good job, then," he answers. His chillingly calm voice is piercing through every bone in her body.

"I'll try again. *That's right!*"

2

MAY 2012

She had never been more beautiful than in this exact moment. No woman ever had. So fragile, her skin so pale it almost looked bluish. The man who called himself the Snakecharmer stared at her body. It was still in the bathtub. He was still panting from the exertion, his hands shaking and hurting from strangling the girl. He felt so aroused in this moment, staring at the dead body. It was the most fascinating thing in the world. How the body simply ceased to function. And almost as fascinating was what followed next. The human decaying process. It wasn't something new. Fascination with death had occurred all throughout human history, characterized by obsessions with death and all things related to death. The Egyptians mummified their dead. He had always wished he could do the same. Keep his dead forever and ever. He remembered as a child how he would sometimes lie down in front of the mirror and try to lie completely still and look at himself, imagining he was looking at a dead body. He would capture cats and kill them and keep them in his room, just to watch what would happen to them. He wanted so badly to stop the decaying process, he wanted them to remain the same always and never leave.

The Snakecharmer stared at the girl with fascination in his eyes. He caught his breath and calmed down again. He still felt the adrenalin rushing through his veins while he finished washing the girl. He washed away all the dirt, all the smells on her body. He reached down and cleaned her thoroughly between her legs. Scrubbed her to make sure he got all the dirt away, all the filth and impurities.

Then, he dried her with a towel before he pulled her onto the bathroom floor. His companions, his two pet Coral snakes, were sliding across her dead body. He grabbed one and let it slide across his arm while petting it. Then he knelt next to the girl and stroked her gently across her hair, making sure it wasn't in her face. Her blue eyes stared into the ceiling.

"Now, you'll never leave," he whispered.

With his cellphone, he took a picture of her naked body. That was his mummification. His way to always cherish the moment. To always remember. He never wanted to forget how beautiful she was.

He dried her with a towel. He brushed her brown hair with gentle strokes. He took yet another picture before he lifted her up and carried her into the bedroom, where he placed her in a chair, then sat in front of her and placed his head in her lap.

They would stay like this until she started to smell.

PART II

I GUESS IF YOU SAY SO

3

JANUARY 2015

He took the dog out in the yard and shut the door carefully behind him, making sure he didn't make a sound to wake up his sleeping parents. It was Monday, but they had been very loud last night. The kitchen counter was still covered with empty bottles.

At first, Ben had waited patiently in the living room, watching a couple of shows on TV, waiting for his parents to wake up. When the clock passed nine, he knew he wouldn't make it to school that day either, and that was too bad because they had a field trip to the zoo today and Ben had been looking forward to it. When they still hadn't shown up at ten o'clock, he decided the dog had to go out. The old Labrador kept sitting by the door and scraping on it. It had to go.

So, Ben took Bobby out in the backyard. He had to go with him. The yard ended at the canal, and Bobby had more than once jumped into the water. Ben had to keep an eye on him to make sure he didn't do it again. It had been such a mess last time, since the dog couldn't climb back up over the seawall on his own, so Ben's dad had to jump into the blurry water and carry the dog out.

The dog quickly gave in to nature and did his business. Ben had a plastic bag that he picked it up with and threw it in the trash can behind the house.

It was a beautiful day out. One of those clear days with a blue sky and not a cloud anywhere on the horizon. The wind was blowing out of the north and had been for two days, making the air drier. For once, Ben's shirt didn't stick to his body.

He threw the ball a few times for the dog to get some exercise. Ben could smell the ocean, even though he lived on the back side of the barrier island. When it was quiet, he could even hear it too. The waves had to be good. If he wasn't too sick from drinking last night, his dad might take him surfing.

Ben really hoped he would.

It had been months since his dad last took him to the beach. He never seemed to have time anymore. Sometimes, Ben would take his bike and ride down there by himself, but it was never as much fun as when the entire family went. They never seemed to do much together anymore. Ben wondered if it had anything to do with what happened to his baby sister a year ago. He never understood exactly what had happened. He just knew she didn't wake up one morning when their mother went to pick her up from her crib. Then his parents cried and cried for days and they had held a big funeral. But the crying hadn't stopped for a long time. Not until it was replaced with a lot of sleeping and his parents staying up all night, and all the empty bottles that Ben often cleaned up from the kitchen and put in the recycling bin.

Bobby brought back the ball and placed it at Ben's feet.

He picked it up and threw it again. It landed close to the seawall. Luckily, it didn't fall in. Bobby ran to get it, then placed it at Ben's feet again, looking at him expectantly.

"Really? One more time, then we're done," he said, thinking he'd better get back inside and start cleaning up. He picked up the ball and threw it. The dog stormed after it again and disappeared for a second down the hill leading to the canal. Ben couldn't see him.

"Bobby?" he yelled. "Come on, boy. We need to get back inside."

He stared in the direction of the canal. He couldn't see the bottom of the yard. He had no idea if Bobby had jumped in the water again. His heart started to pound. He would have to wake up his dad if he did. He was the only one who could get Bobby out of the water.

Ben stood frozen for a few seconds until he heard the sound of Bobby's collar, and a second later spotted his black dog running towards him with his tongue hanging out of his mouth.

"Bobby!" Ben said. He bent down and petted his dog and best friend. "You scared me, buddy. You forgot the ball. Well, we'll have to get that later. Now, let's go back inside and see if Mom and Dad are awake."

Ben grabbed the handle and opened the door. He let Bobby go in first.

"Mom?" he called.

But there was no answer. They were probably still asleep. Ben found some dog food in the cabinet and pulled the bag out. He spilled on the floor when he filled Bobby's tray. He had no idea how much the dog needed, so he made sure to give him enough, and poured till the bowl over-flowed. Ben found a garbage bag under the sink and had removed some of the bottles, when Bobby suddenly started growling. The dog ran to the bottom of the stairs and barked. Ben found this to be strange. It was very unlike Bobby to act this way.

"What's the matter, boy? Are Mom and Dad awake?"

The dog kept barking and growling.

"Stop it!" Ben yelled, knowing how much his dad hated it when Bobby barked. "Bad dog."

But Bobby didn't stop. He moved closer and closer to the stairs and kept barking until the dog finally ran up the stairs.

"No! Bobby!" Ben yelled. "Come back down here!"

Ben stared up the stairs after the dog, wondering if he dared to go up there. His dad always got so mad if he went upstairs when they were sleeping. He wasn't allowed up there until they got out of bed. But, if he found Bobby up there, his dad would get really mad. Probably talk about getting rid of him again.

He's my best friend. Don't take my friend away.

"Bobby," he whispered. "Come back down here."

Ben's heart was racing in his chest. There wasn't a sound coming from upstairs. Ben held his breath, not knowing what to do. The last thing he wanted on a day like today was to make his dad angry. He expected his dad to start yelling any second now.

Oh no, what if he jumps into their bed? Dad is going to get so mad. He's gonna get real mad at Bobby.

"Bobby?" Ben whispered a little louder.

There was movement on the stairs, the black lab peeked his head out, then ran down the stairs.

"There you are," Ben said with relief. Bobby ran past him and sprang up on the couch.

"What do you have in your mouth? Not one of mom's shoes again."

It didn't look like it was big enough to be a shoe. Ben walked closer, thinking if it was a pair of Mommy's panties again, then the dog was dead. He reached down and grabbed the dog's mouth, then opened it and pulled out whatever it was. He looked down with a small shriek at what had come out of the dog's mouth. He felt nauseated, like the time when he had the stomach-bug and spent the entire night in the bathroom. Only this was worse.

It's a finger. A finger wearing Mommy's ring!

4

JANUARY 2015

"Hit the road, Jack, and don't you come back no more no more no more."

The children's voices were screaming more than singing on the bus. I preferred *Wheels on the Bus,* but the kids thought it was oh so fun, since my name was Jack and I was actually driving the bus. I had volunteered to drive them to the Brevard Zoo for their field trip today. Two of the children, the pretty blonde twins in the back named Abigail and Austin, were mine. A boy and a girl. Just started Kindergarten six months ago. I could hardly believe how fast time passed. Everybody told me it would, but still. It was hard to believe.

I was thirty-five and a single dad of three children. My wife, Arianna, ran out on us four years ago...when the twins were almost two years old. It was too much, she told me. She couldn't cope with the children or me. She especially had a hard time taking care of Emily. Emily was my ex-partner's daughter. My ex-partner, Lisa, was shot on duty ten years ago during a chase in downtown Miami. The shooter was never captured, and it haunted me daily. I took Emily in after her mother died. What else could I have done? I felt guilty for what had happened to her mother. I was supposed to have protected my partner. Plus, the girl didn't know her father. Lisa never told anyone who he was; she didn't have any of her parents or siblings left, except for a homeless brother who was in no condition to take care of a child. So, I got custody and decided to give Emily the best life I could. She was six when I took her in, sixteen now, and at an age where it was hard for anyone to love you, besides your mom and dad. I tried hard to be both for her. Not always with much success. The fact was, I had no idea what it was like to be a black teenage girl.

Personally, I believed Arianna had depression after the birth of the twins, but she never let me close enough to talk about it. She cried for months after the twins were born, then one day out of the blue, she told me she had to go. That she couldn't stay or it would end up killing her. I cried and begged her to stay, but there was nothing I could do. She had made up her mind. She was going back upstate, and that was all I needed to know. I shouldn't look for her, she said.

"Are you coming back?" I asked, my voice breaking. I couldn't believe anyone would leave her own children.

"I don't know, Jack."

"But...The children? They need you? They need their mother?"

"I can't be the mother you want me to be, Jack. I'm just not cut out for it. I'm sorry."

Then she left. Just like that. I had no idea how to explain it to the kids, but somehow I did. As soon as they started asking questions, I told them their mother had left and that I believed she was coming back one day. Some, maybe a lot of people, including my mother, might have told me it was insane to tell them that she might be coming back, but that's what I did. I couldn't bear the thought of them growing up with the knowledge that their own mother didn't want them. I couldn't bear for Emily to know that she was part of the reason why Arianna had left us, left the twins mother-less. I just couldn't. I had to leave them with some sort of hope. And maybe I needed to believe it too. I needed to believe that she hadn't just abandoned us...that she had some stuff she needed to work out and soon she would be back. At least for the twins. They needed their mother and asked for her often. It was getting harder and harder for me to believe she was coming back for them. But I still said she would.

And there they were.

On the back seat of the bus, singing along with their classmates, happier than most of them. Mother or no mother, I had provided a good life for them in our little town of Cocoa Beach. As a detective working for the Brevard County Sheriff's Office, working their homicide unit, I had lots of spare time and they had their grandparents close by. They received all the love in the world from me and their grandparents, who loved them to death (and let them get away with just about anything).

Some might think they were spoiled brats, but to me they were the love of my life, the light, the...the...

What the heck were they doing in the back?

I hit the brakes a little too hard at the red light. All the kids on the bus fell forwards. The teacher, Mrs. Allen, whined and held on to her purse.

"Abigail and Austin!" I thundered through the bus. "Stop that right now!"

The twins grinned and looked at one another, then continued to smear chocolate on each other's faces. Chocolate from those small boxes with Nutella and sticks you dipped in it. Boxes their grandmother had given them for snack, even though I told her it had to be healthy.

"Now!" I yelled.

"Sorry, Dad," they yelled in unison.

"Well...wipe that off or..."

I never made it any further before the phone in my pocket vibrated. I pulled it out and started driving again as the light turned green.

"Ryder. We need you. I spoke with Ron and he told me you would be assisting us. We desperately need your help."

It was the head of the Cocoa Beach Police Department. Weasel, we called her. I didn't know why. Maybe it had to do with the fact that her name was Weslie Seal. Maybe it was just because she kind of looked like a weasel because her body was long and slender, but her legs very short. Ron Harper was the county sheriff and my boss.

"Yes? When?"

"Now."

"But...I'm..."

"This is big. We need you now."

"If you say so. I'll get there as fast as I can," I said, and turned off towards the entrance to the zoo. The kids all screamed with joy when they saw the sign. Mrs. Allen shushed them.

"What, are you running a day-care now? Not that I have the time to care. Everything is upside down around here. We have a dead body. I'll text you the address. Meet you there."

5

APRIL 1984

Annie was getting ready. She was putting on make-up with her room-mate Julia, while listening to Michael Jackson's *Thriller* and singing into their hairbrushes. They were nineteen, in college, and heading for trouble, as Annie's father always said.

Annie wanted to be a teacher.

"Are you excited?" Julia asked. "You think he's going to be there?"

"He," was Tim. He was the talk of the campus and the guy they all desired. He was tall, blond, and a quarterback. He was perfect. And he had his eye on Annie.

"I hope so," Annie said, and put on her jacket with the shoulder pads. "He asked me to come; he'd better be."

She looked at her friend, wondering why Tim hadn't chosen Julia instead. She was much prettier.

"Shall we?" Julia asked and opened the door. They were both wearing heavy make-up and acid-washed jeans.

Annie was nervous as they walked to the party. She had never been to a party in a fraternity house before. She had been thrilled when Tim came up to her in the library where she hung out most of the time and told her there was a party at the house and asked if she was going to come.

"Sure," she had replied, while blushing.

"This is it," Julia said, as they approached the house. Kids a few years older than them were hanging out on the porch, while loud music spilled out through the open windows. Annie had butterflies in her stomach as they went up the steps to the front of the house and entered, elbowing themselves through the crowd.

The noise was intense. People were drinking and smoking everywhere. Some were already making out on a couch. And it wasn't even nine o'clock yet.

"Let's get something to drink," Julia yelled through the thick clamor. "Have you loosen up a little."

Julia came back with two cups, and...Tim. "Look who I found," she said. "He was asking for you."

Annie grabbed the plastic cup and didn't care what it contained; she gulped it down in such a hurry she forgot to breathe. Tim was staring at her with that handsome smile of his. Then, he leaned over, put his hand on her shoulder, and whispered. "Glad you came."

Annie blushed and felt warmth spread through her entire body from the palm of Tim's hand on her shoulder. She really liked him. She really, really liked him.

"It's very loud in here. Do you want to go somewhere?" he asked.

Annie knew she wasn't the smartest among girls. Her mother had always told her so. She knew Tim, who was pre-med, would never be impressed with her conversational skills or her wits. If she was to dazzle him, it had to be in another way.

"Sure," she said.

"Let me get us some drinks first," Tim said and disappeared.

Julia smiled and grabbed Annie's shoulders. "You got him, girl." Then she corrected Annie's hair and wiped a smear of mascara from under her eyes.

"There. Now you're perfect. Remember. Don't think. You always overthink everything. Just be you. Just go with the flow, all right? Laugh at his jokes, but not too hard. Don't tell him too much about yourself; stay mysterious. And, whatever you do...don't sleep with him. You hear me? He won't respect you if you jump into bed with him right away. You have to play hard to get."

Annie stared at Julia. She had never had sex with anyone before, and she certainly wasn't going to now. Not yet. She had been saving herself for the right guy, and maybe Tim was it, but she wasn't going to decide that tonight. She didn't even want to.

"I'd never do that," she said with a scoff. "I'm not THAT stupid."

6

JANUARY 2015

Weasel was standing outside the house as I drove up and parked the school bus on the street. The house on West Bay Drive was blocked by four police cars and lots of police tape. I saw several of my colleagues walking around in the yard. Weasel spotted me and approached. She was wearing tight black jeans, a belt with a big buckle, a white shirt, and black blazer. She looked to be in her thirties, but I knew she had recently turned forty.

"What the...?" she said with a grin, looking at the bus. She had that raspy rawness to her voice, and I always wondered if she could sing. I pictured her as a country singer. She gave out that tough vibe.

"Don't ask," I said. "What have we got?"

"Homicide," Weasel answered. "Victim is female. Laura Bennett, thirty-two, Mom of Ben, five years old. The husband's name is Brandon Bennett."

My heart dropped. I knew the boy. He was in the twins' class. I couldn't believe it. I had moved to Cocoa Beach from Miami in 2008 and never been called out to a homicide in my own town. Our biggest problems around here were usually tourists on spring break jumping in people's pools and Jacuzzis and leaving beer cans, or the youngsters having bonfires on the beach and burning people's chairs and leaving trash.

But, murder? That was a first for me in Cocoa Beach. I had been called out to drug related homicides in the beach-side area before, but that was mostly further down south in Satellite Beach and Indialantic, but never this far up north.

"It's bad," Weasel said. "I have close to no experience with this type of thing, but you do. We need all your Miami-experience now. Show me what you've got."

I nodded and followed her into the house. It was located on a canal leading to the Banana River, like most of the houses on the back side of the island. The house had a big pebble-coated pool area with two waterfalls, a slide, and a spa overlooking the river. The perfect setting for Florida living, the real estate ad would say. With the huge palm trees, it looked like true paradise. Until you stepped inside.

The inside was pure hell.

It was a long time since I had been on a murder scene, but the Weasel was right. I was the only one with lots of experience in this field. I spent eight years in downtown Miami, covering Overtown, the worst neighborhood in the town, as part of the homicide unit. My specialty was the killer's psychology. I was a big deal back then. But when I met Arianna and she became pregnant with the twins, I was done. It was suddenly too dangerous. We left Miami to get away from it. We moved to Cocoa Beach, where my parents lived, to be closer to my family and to get away from murder.

Now, it had followed me here. It made me feel awful. I hated to see the town's innocence go like this.

My colleagues from the Cocoa Beach Police Department greeted me with nods as we walked through the living room, overlooking the yard with the pool. I knew all of them. They seemed a little confused. For most of them, it was a first. Officer Joel Hall looked pale.

"Joel was first man here," Weasel said.

"How are you doing, Joel?" I asked.

"Been better."

"So, tell me what happened."

Joel sniffled and wiped his nose on his sleeve.

"We got a call from the boy. He told us his mother had been killed. He found her finger...well, the dog had it in his mouth. He didn't dare to go upstairs. He called 911 immediately. I was on patrol close by, so I drove down here."

"So, what did you find?"

"The boy and the dog were waiting outside the house. He was hysterical, kept telling me his parents were dead. Then, he showed me the finger. I tried to calm him down and tell him I would go look and to stay outside. I walked up and found the mother..." Joel sniffled again. He took in a deep breath.

"Take your time, Joel," I said, and put my hand on his shoulder. Joel finally caved in and broke down.

"You better see it with your own eyes," Weasel said. "But brace yourself."

I followed her up the stairs of the house, where the medical examiners were already taking samples.

"The kid said his parents were dead. What about the dad?" I asked. "You only said one homicide."

"The dad's fine. But, hear this," Weasel said. "He claims he was asleep the entire time. He's been taken to the hospital to see a doctor. He kept claiming he felt dizzy and had blurred vision. I had to have a doctor look at him before we talk to him. The boy is with him. Didn't want to leave his side. The dog is there too. Jim and Marty took them there. I don't want him to run. He's our main suspect so far."

We walked down the hallway till we reached the bedroom. "Brace yourself," Weasel repeated, right before we walked inside.

I sucked in my breath. Then I froze.

"It looks like he was dismembering her," Weasel said. "He cut off all the fingers on her right hand, one by one, then continued on to the toes on her foot."

I felt disgusted by the sight. I held a hand to cover my mouth, not because it smelled, but because I always became sick to my stomach when facing a dead body. Especially one that was mutilated. I never got used to it. I kneeled next to the woman lying on the floor. I examined her face and eyes, lifted her eyelids, then looked closely at her body.

"There's hardly any blood. No bruises either," I said. "I say she was strangled first, then he did the dismembering. My guess is he was disturbed. He was about to cut her into bits and pieces, but he stopped. "I sniffed the body and looked at the Weasel, who seemed disgusted by my motion. "The kill might have happened in the shower. She has been washed recently. Maybe he drowned her."

I walked into the bathroom and approached the tub. I ran a finger along the sides. "Look." I showed her my finger. "There's still water on the sides. It's been used recently."

"So, you think she was killed in the bathtub? Strangulation, you say? But there are no marks on her neck or throat?"

"Look at her eyes. Petechiae. Tiny red spots due to ruptured capillaries. They are a signature injury of strangulation. She has them under the eyelids. He didn't use his hands. He was being gentle."

Weasel looked appalled. "Gentle? How can you say he was gentle? He cut off her fingers?"

"Yes, but look how methodical he was. All the parts are intact. Not a bruise on any of them. Not a drop of blood. They are all placed neatly next to one another. It's a declaration of love."

Weasel looked confused. She grumbled. "I don't see much love in any of all this, that's for sure. All I see is a dead woman, who someone tried to chop up. And now I want you to find out who did it."

I chuckled. "So, the dad tells us he was sleeping?" I asked.

Weasel shrugged. "Apparently, he was drunk last night. They had friends over. It got a little heavy, according to the neighbors. Loud music and loud voices. But that isn't new with these people."

"On a Sunday night in a nice neighborhood like this?" I asked, surprised.

"Apparently."

"It's a big house. Right on the river. Snug Harbor is one of the most expensive neighborhoods around here. What do the parents do for a living?"

"Nothing, I've been told. They live off the family's money. The deceased's father was a very famous writer. He died ten years ago. The kids have been living off of the inheritance and the royalties for years since."

"Anyone I know, the writer?"

"Probably," she said. "A local hero around here. John Platt."

"John Platt?" I said. "I've certainly heard of him. I didn't know he used to live around here. Wasn't he the guy who wrote all those thriller-novels that were made into movies later on?"

"Yes, that was him. He has sold more than 100 million books worldwide. His books are still topping the bestseller lists."

"Didn't he recently publish a new book or something?"

Weasel nodded. "They found an old unpublished manuscript of his on his computer, which they published. I never understood how those things work, but I figure they think, if he wrote it, then it's worth a lot of money even if he trashed it."

I stared at the dead halfway-dismembered body on the floor, then back at the Weasel.

I sighed. "I guess we better talk to this heavily sleeping dad first."

JANUARY 2015

"Who was that guy you talked to last night?"

Joe walked into the kitchen. Shannon was cutting up oranges to make juice. She sensed he was right behind her, but she didn't turn to look at him. Last night was still in her head. The humming noise of the voices, the music, the laughter. Her head was hurting from a little too much alcohol. His question made everything inside of her freeze.

"Who do you mean?" she asked. "I talked to a lot of people. That was kind of the idea with the party after my concert. For me to meet with the press and important people in the business. That's the way it always is. You know how it goes. It's a big part of my job."

He put his hand on her shoulder. A shiver ran up her spine. She closed her eyes.

Not now. Please not now.

"Look at me when you're talking to me," he said.

She took in a deep breath, then put on a smile; the same smile she used when the press asked her to pose for pictures, the same smile she put on for her manager, her record label, and her friends when they asked her about the bruises on her back, followed by the sentence:

"Just me being clumsy again."

Shannon turned and looked at Joe. His eyes were black with fury. Her body shrunk and her smile froze.

"I saw the way you were looking at that guy. Don't you think I saw that?" Joe asked. "You know what I think? I think you like going to these parties they throw in your honor. I think you enjoy all the men staring at you, wishing you were theirs, wanting to fuck your brains out. I see it in their eyes and I see it in yours as well. You like it."

It was always the same. Joe couldn't stand the fact that Shannon was the famous one...that she was the one everyone wanted to talk to, and after a party like the one yesterday, he always lost his temper with her. Because he felt left out, because there was no one looking at him, talking to him, asking him questions with interest. He hated the fact that Shannon was the one with a career, when all he had ever dreamt of was to be singing in sold out stadiums like she did.

They had started out together. Each with just a guitar under their arm, working small clubs and bars in Texas, then later they moved on to Nashville, where country musicians were made. They played the streets together, and then got small gigs in bars, and later small concert venues around town. But when a record label contacted them one day after a concert, they were only interested in her. They only wanted Shannon King. Since then, Joe had been living in the shadow of his wife, and that didn't become him well. For years, she had made excuses for him, telling herself he was going through a rough time; he was just hurting because he wasn't going anywhere with his music. The only thing Joe had going for him right now was the fact that he was stronger than Shannon.

But as the years had passed, it was getting harder and harder for her to come up with new excuses, new explanations. Especially now that they had a child together. A little girl who was beginning to ask questions.

"Joe...I...I don't know what you're talking about. I talked to a lot of people last night. I'm tired and now I really want to get some breakfast."

"Did you just take a tone with me. Did ya'? Am I so insignificant in your life that you don't even talk to me with respect, huh? You don't even look at me when we're at your precious after party. Nobody cares about me. Everyone just wants to talk to the *biiig* star, Shannon King," he said, mocking her.

"You're being ridiculous."

"Am I? Did you even think about me once last night? Did you? I left at eleven-thirty. You never even noticed. You never even texted me and asked where I was."

Shannon blushed. He was right. She hadn't thought about him even once. She had been busy answering questions from the press and talking about her tour. Everyone had been pulling at her; there simply was no time to think about him. Why couldn't he understand that?

"I thought so," Joe said. Then, he slapped her.

Shannon went stumbling backward against the massive granite counter. She hurt her back in the fall. Shannon whimpered, then got up on her feet again with much effort. Her cheek burned like hell. A little blood ran from the corner of her mouth. She wiped it off.

Careful what you say, Shannon. Careful not to upset him further. Remember what happened last time. He's not well. He is hurting. Careful not to hurt him any more.

But she knew it was too late. She knew once he crossed that line into that area where all thinking ceased to exist, it was too late. She could appeal to his sensitivity as much as she wanted to. She could try and explain herself and tell him she was sorry, but it didn't help. If anything, it only made everything worse.

His eyes were bulging and his jaws clenched. His right eye had that tick in it that only showed when he was angry.

You got to get out of here.

"Joe, please, I..."

A fist throbbed through the air and smashed into her face.

Quick. Run for the phone.

She could see it. It was on the breakfast bar. She would have to spring for it. Shannon jumped to the side and managed to avoid his next fist, then slipped on the small rug on the kitchen floor, got back up in a hurry, and rushed to reach out for the phone.

Call 911. Call the police.

Her legs were in the air and she wasn't running anymore. He had grabbed her by the hair, and now he was pulling her backwards. He yanked her towards him, and she screamed in pain, cursing her long blonde hair that she used to love so much...that the world loved and put on magazine covers.

"You cheating lying bitch!" he screamed, while pulling her across the floor.

He lifted her up, then threw her against the kitchen counter. It blew out the air from her lungs. She couldn't scream anymore. She was panting for air and wheezing for him to stop. She was bleeding from her nose. Joe came closer, then leaned over her and, with his hand, he corrected his hair. His precious hair that had always meant so much to him, that he was always fixing and touching to make sure it was perfect, which it ironically never was.

"No one disrespects me. Do you hear me? Especially not you. You're a nobody. Do you understand? You would be nothing if it wasn't for me," he yelled, then lifted his clenched fist one more time. When it smashed into Shannon's face again and again, she finally let herself drift into a darkness so deep she couldn't feel anything anymore.

"Hi there. Ben, is it?" I asked.

The boy was sitting next to his dad in the hospital bed, the dog sleeping by his feet.

"He won't leave his dad's side," Marty said.

Ben looked up at me with fear in his eyes. "It's okay, Ben," I said, and kneeled in front of him. "We can talk here."

"I know you," Ben said. "You're Austin and Abigail's dad."

"That's right. And you're in their class. I remember you. Say, weren't you supposed to be at the zoo today?"

Ben nodded with a sad expression.

"Well, there'll be other times," I said. I paused while Ben looked at his father, who was sleeping.

"He's completely out cold," Marty said. "He was complaining that he couldn't control his arms and legs, had spots before his eyes, and he felt dizzy and nauseated. Guess it was really heavy last night."

I looked at the very pale dad. "Or maybe it was something else," I said.

"What do you mean?"

I looked closer at the dad.

"Did you talk to him?"

"Only a few words. When I asked about last night, he kept saying he didn't remember what happened, that he didn't know where he was. He kept asking me what time it was. Even after I had just told him."

"Hm."

"What?" Marty asked.

"Did they run his blood work?" I asked.

"No. I told them it wasn't necessary. He was just hung over. The doctor looked at him quickly and agreed. We agreed to let him to sleep it off. He seemed like he was still drunk when he talked to us."

"Is my dad sick, Mr. Ryder?" Ben asked.

I looked at the boy and smiled. "No, son, but I am afraid your dad has been poisoned."

"Poisoned?" Marty asked. "What on earth do you mean?"

"Dizziness, confusion, blurry vision, difficulty talking, nausea, difficulty controlling your movements all are symptoms of Rohypnol poisoning. Must have been ingested to have this big of an affect. Especially with alcohol."

"Roofied?" Marty laughed. "Who on earth in their right mind would give a grown man a rape drug?"

"Someone who wanted to kill him and his wife," I said.

I walked into the hallway and found a nurse and asked her to make sure they tested Brandon Bennett for the drug in his blood. Then, I called the medical examiner and told them to check the wife's blood as well. Afterwards, I returned to talk to Ben.

"So, Ben, I know this is a difficult time for you, but I would be really happy if you could help me out by talking a little about last night. Can you help me out here?"

Ben wiped his eyes and looked at me. His face was swollen from crying. Then he nodded. I opened my arms. "Come here, buddy. You look like you could use a good bear hug."

Ben hesitated, then looked at his dad, who was still out cold, before he finally gave in and let me hug him. I held him in my arms, the way I held my own children when they were sad. The boy finally cried.

"It's okay," I whispered. "Your dad will be fine."

My words felt vague compared to what the little boy had seen this morning, how his world had been shaken up. His dad was probably going to be fine, but he would never see his mother again, and the real question was whether the boy would ever be fine again?

He wept in my arms for a few minutes, then pulled away and wiped his nose on his sleeve. "Do you promise to catch the guy that killed my mother?" he asked.

I sighed. "I can promise I'll do my best. How about that?"

Ben thought about it for a little while, then nodded with a sniffle.

"Okay. What do you want to know?" he asked.

"Who came to your house last night? I heard your parents had guests. Who were they?"

9

APRIL 1984

Tim took Annie down to the lake behind campus, where they sat down. The grass was moist from the sprinklers. Annie felt self-conscious with the way Tim stared at her. It was a hot night out. The cicadas were singing; Annie was sweating in her small dress. Her skin felt clammy.

Tim finally broke the silence.

"Has anyone ever told you how incredibly beautiful you are?"

Annie's head was spinning from her drink. The night was intoxicating, the sounds, the smell, the moist air hugging her. She shook her head. Her eyes stared at the grass. She felt her cheeks blushing.

"No."

"Really?" Tim said. "I find that very hard to believe."

Annie giggled, then sipped her drink. She really liked Tim. She could hardly believe she was really here with him.

"Look at the moon," he said and pointed.

It was a full moon. It was shining almost as bright as

daylight. Its light hit the lake. Annie took in a deep breath, taking in the moment.

"It's beautiful," she said with a small still voice. She was afraid of talking too much, since he would only realize she wasn't smart, and then he might regret being with her.

Just go with the flow.

"I loathe Florida," Tim said. "I hate these warm nights. I hate how sweaty I always am. I'm especially sick of Orlando. When I'm done here, I'm getting out of this state. I wanna go up north. Don't you?"

Annie shrugged. She had lived all her life in Florida. Thirty minutes north of Orlando, to be exact. Born and raised in Windermere. Her parents still lived there, and that was where she was planning on going back once she had her degree. Annie had never thought about going anywhere else.

"I guess it's nice up north as well," she said, just to please him.

Tim laughed, then looked at her with those intense eyes once again. It made her uncomfortable. But part of her liked it as well. A big part.

"Can I kiss you?" he asked.

Annie blushed. She really wanted him to. Then she nodded. Tim smiled, then leaned over and put his lips on top of hers. Annie felt the dizziness from the drink. It was buzzing in her head. The kiss made her head spin, and when Tim pressed her down on the moist grass, she let him. He crawled on top of her, and with deep moans kept kissing her lips, then her cheeks, her ears, and her neck. Annie felt like laughing because it tickled so much, but she held it back to not ruin anything. Tim liked her and it made her happy.

"Boy, you're hot," he said, groaning, as he kissed her

throat and moved further down her body. He grinned and started to open her dress, taking one button at a time. Annie felt insecure. What was he going to do next?

Tim pulled the dress open and looked at her bra, then he ripped it off.

"Ouch," Annie said. She tried to cover her breasts with her arms, but Tim soon grabbed them and pulled them to her sides. He held her down while kissing her breasts. He groaned while sucking on her nipples. Annie wasn't sure if she liked it or not. He was being a little rough, and she was afraid of going too far with him.

Whatever you do, don't sleep with him. No matter what.

"Stop," she mumbled, when he pulled the dress off completely and grabbed her panties. Tim stopped. He stared at Annie. She felt bad. Had she scared him away? Was he ever going to see her again if she didn't let him?

No matter what.

No. She wasn't ready for this. She had saved herself. This wasn't how it was supposed to happen. Not like this. Not here.

"I want to go home," Annie said.

Tim smiled and tilted his head, then leaned over and whispered in her ear. "Not yet, sweetheart, not yet."

He stroked her face gently and kissed her cheeks, while she fought and tried to get him off her body. In the distance, she heard voices, and soon she felt hands on her body, hands touching her, hands slapping her face. She felt so dizzy and everything became a blur of faces, laughing voices, cheering voices, hands everywhere, groping her, touching her, hurting her. And then the pain followed.

The excruciating pain.

ORDER YOUR COPY TODAY!

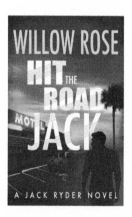

Made in the USA
Coppell, TX
06 December 2020

43448244R00080